DINOSAURS
IN YOUR BACKYARD

Hugh Brewster
Illustrated by Alan Barnard

ABRAMS BOOKS FOR YOUNG READERS
NEW YORK

DINOSAURS

When we look at dinosaurs in the museum, we imagine them alive. Maybe you'd like to add flesh to their bones and see them roaring, baring their enormous teeth. Perhaps you'd even like to see them come to life and go charging through the building! (You know that this couldn't happen, of course, since dinosaurs died out millions of years ago.)

But maybe you don't know just how many of these amazing creatures once lived right here in the USA. More than 85 different kinds of dinosaurs have been found in North America — but there could have been thousands more. Scientists think that only a small number of all the dinosaur species that ever lived have been discovered. We only know about the dinosaurs that left behind bones or footprints that hardened into stone fossils.

Maybe dinosaurs once lived where you live. Huge herds of giant, snorting creatures could have stomped right through your backyard!

AMERICA

WHEN THE DINOSAURS RULED

Seventy million years ago, a shallow inland seaway ran from the Arctic Ocean right down to the Gulf of Mexico (inset, above). Along its shores many different kinds of dinosaurs feasted on the lush greenery and flowering plants that grew in its swampy river deltas. The climate was mostly wet and tropical — even as far north as Alaska.

Finding *Bambiraptor*

When 14-year-old Wes Linster was hiking near Montana's Glacier National Park in 1995, he found a skeleton on a high hill. "I bolted down the hill to get my mom because I knew I shouldn't be messing with it," he remembers.

His discovery led to the excavation of a 75-million-year-old bird-like dinosaur named *Bambiraptor*. Only 2.3 feet in length, *Bambiraptor* provides an important link in understanding the evolution of dinosaurs into birds (see p. 24).

Bambiraptor

Did Dinosaurs Only Live in the West?

It's likely that dinosaurs lived all over North America. More fossils have been found in western states like Montana and Utah because the rocks there date from the time of the dinosaurs and conditions were best there for fossilizing bones.

The Dinosaur in the Bridge

When a stone bridge in South Manchester, Connecticut, was demolished in 1969, paleontologist John Ostrom was excited. He thought that the stone blocks that were used to build the bridge in 1884 might contain some missing dinosaur bones. In the blocks, Ostrom did find fossil bones from an *Ammosaurus major* ("greater sand reptile"), a 13-foot dinosaur that lived about 180 million years ago. The fossils were added to the rest of the skeleton, which was already at Yale's Peabody Museum.

Dino Tracks

Dinosaur State Park in Rocky Hill, Connecticut, has fossilized footprints, called *Eubrontes,* that were made by giant, three-toed creatures 200 million years ago.

The First Dinosaur Skeleton

In 1858 a fossil collector named William Parker Foulke was visiting Haddonfield, New Jersey. He heard that some gigantic bones had been dug up near there 20 years before. Foulke hired some diggers and uncovered the most complete dinosaur skeleton then known. Named *Hadrosaurus foulkii*, it was put on display at the Philadelphia Academy of Natural Sciences and can still be seen there today.

Hadrosaurus foulkii

Mosasaur

Giant Swimming Reptiles The shallow sea that covered most of the Great Plains and the Southwest swarmed with life (see pp. 8–9). Sharks grew to 25 feet and even some clams could be 36 inches in size. But the reptile that ruled was the 46- to 56-foot-long mosasaur, which had a crocodile's head, a snake-like body, and flippers. Well-preserved skeletons of mosasaurs have been found in South Dakota and western Kansas.

They were some of the largest, fiercest carnivores the world has ever seen. And they roamed through western North America 80 to 65 million years ago. Everybody's favorite scary dino, *Tyrannosaurus rex*, was the king of the "tyrant lizards" — which is just what its name means. As long as a school bus and as heavy as two elephants, *T. rex* had the most powerful bite of any animal that has ever lived. Its huge teeth were serrated like steak knives and could chomp right through flesh and bones.

BIG AND DEADLY
TYRANNOSAURS

Another tyrannosaur, named *Gorgosaurus*, was smaller than *T. rex* but was every bit as vicious. With its long legs it was able to chase down the duck-billed dinosaurs on which it feasted.

If a *T. rex* fought a *Gorgosaurus,* who would win?
Neither, because *Gorgosaurus* died out a million years before *T. rex* came on the scene.

T. REX   VS   GORGOSAURUS

Name Means:
"Tyrant lizard king"
Size: 40 feet long and 15–20 feet tall
Weight: Up to 7.5 tons

Time: 68–65 million years ago
Diet: Meat
Found: Western North America

Name Means:
"Fierce lizard"
Size: 26–30 feet long and 11 feet tall

Weight: 2.7 tons
Time: 72–69 million years ago
Diet: Meat
Found: Western North America

A Gorgosaurus uses its powerful jaws to bring down a duck-billed Hypacrosaurus.

SEA MONSTERS OVER

Huge marine reptiles (which were not dinosaurs) lived over what is now the Great Plains. The long-necked elasmosaur gobbled fish with its powerful jaws and teeth. It could be up to 46 feet long, and over half of that length was its neck. A mosasaur could be up to 10 feet longer and looked like a giant crocodile with flippers. It could snag large fish or even small sharks with its massive teeth.

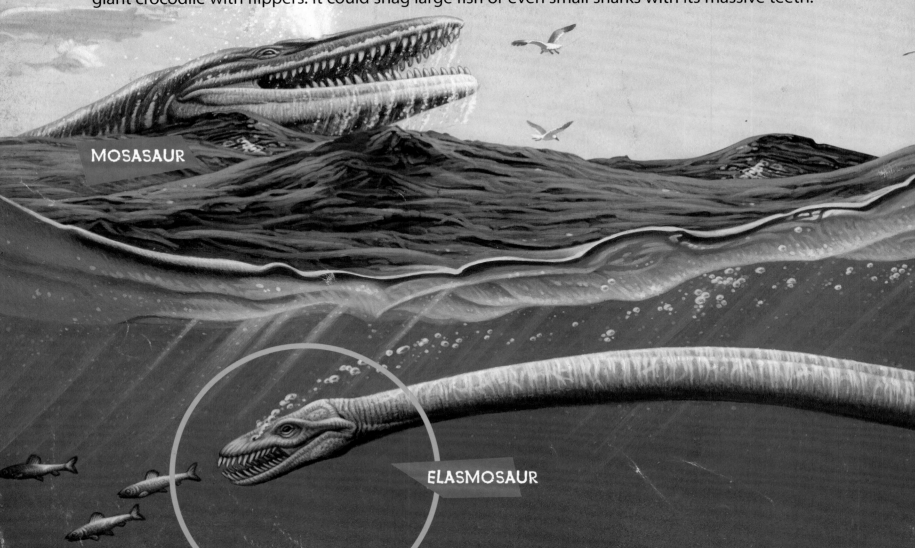

MOSASAUR

ELASMOSAUR

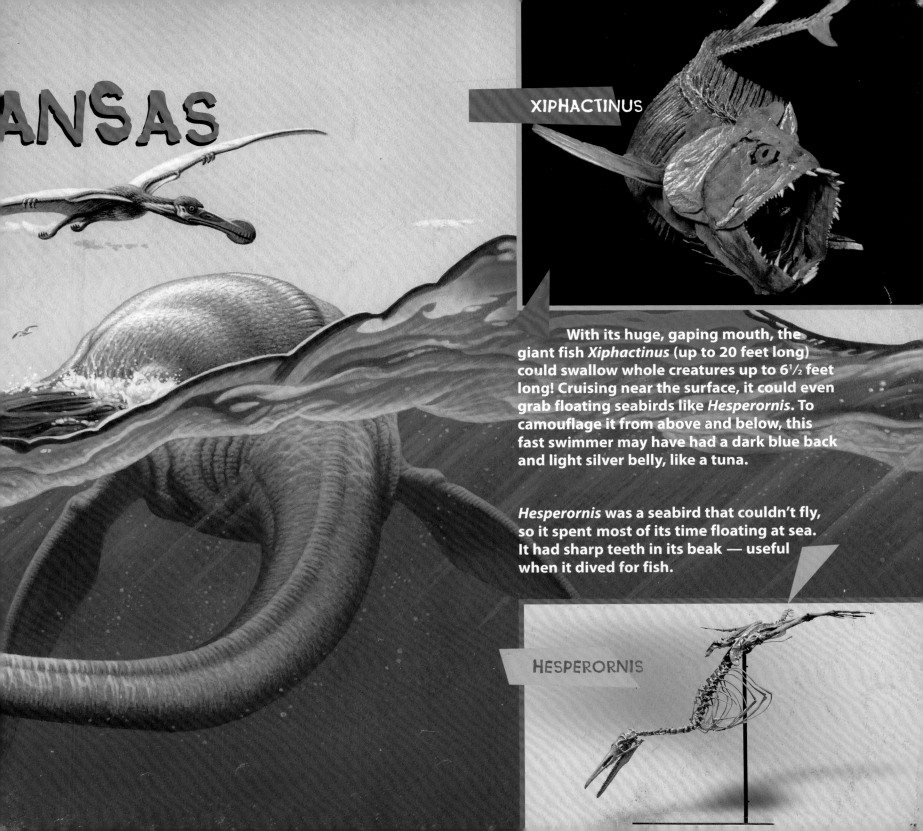

ANSAS

XIPHACTINUS

With its huge, gaping mouth, the giant fish *Xiphactinus* (up to 20 feet long) could swallow whole creatures up to 6½ feet long! Cruising near the surface, it could even grab floating seabirds like *Hesperornis*. To camouflage it from above and below, this fast swimmer may have had a dark blue back and light silver belly, like a tuna.

Hesperornis was a seabird that couldn't fly, so it spent most of its time floating at sea. It had sharp teeth in its beak — useful when it dived for fish.

HESPERORNIS

A WESTERN SHOWDOWN

Screams and roars pierced the dusty air of ancient Colorado. The *Stegosaurus* swung its heavy tail and the *Allosaurus* howled as the 3-foot-long spikes from the tail sank into its neck. Two other allosaurs from the pack came to help. They circled around the stegosaur, whose tail spikes had become firmly stuck in the first allosaur's back. One allosaur ripped the stegosaur's belly with its sharp claws while the other tried to bite its head. The stegosaur was no match for the huge predators and soon toppled, bleeding, on its side. Before long, the three allosaurs gorged greedily on their prey.

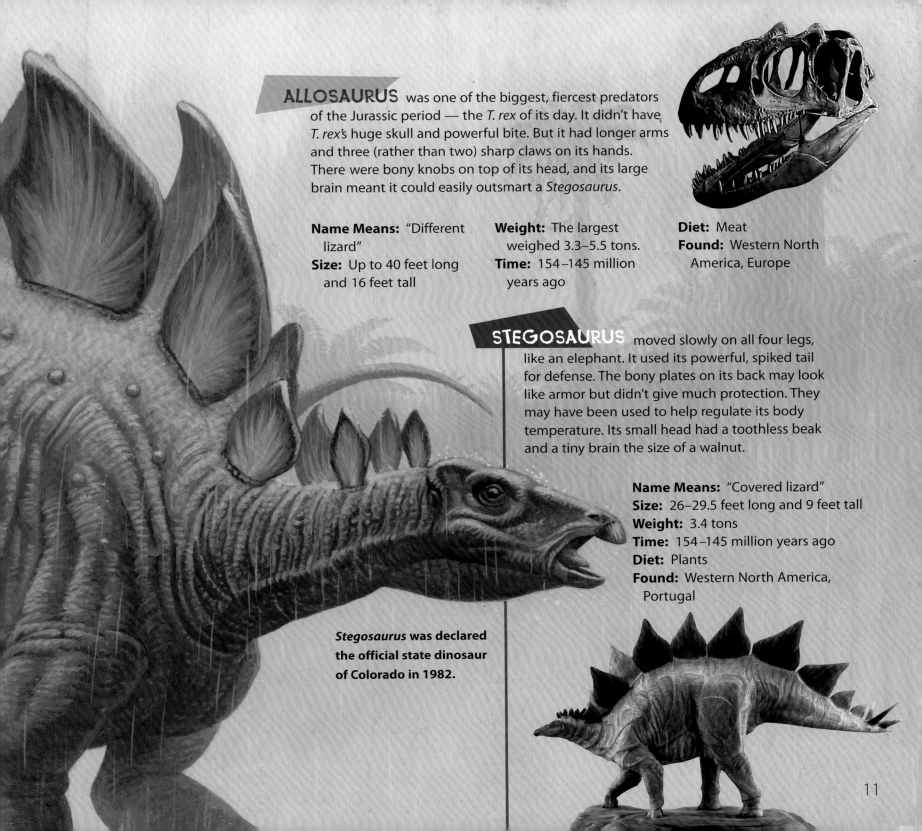

ALLOSAURUS was one of the biggest, fiercest predators of the Jurassic period — the *T. rex* of its day. It didn't have *T. rex*'s huge skull and powerful bite. But it had longer arms and three (rather than two) sharp claws on its hands. There were bony knobs on top of its head, and its large brain meant it could easily outsmart a *Stegosaurus*.

Name Means: "Different lizard"
Size: Up to 40 feet long and 16 feet tall

Weight: The largest weighed 3.3–5.5 tons.
Time: 154–145 million years ago

Diet: Meat
Found: Western North America, Europe

STEGOSAURUS moved slowly on all four legs, like an elephant. It used its powerful, spiked tail for defense. The bony plates on its back may look like armor but didn't give much protection. They may have been used to help regulate its body temperature. Its small head had a toothless beak and a tiny brain the size of a walnut.

Name Means: "Covered lizard"
Size: 26–29.5 feet long and 9 feet tall
Weight: 3.4 tons
Time: 154–145 million years ago
Diet: Plants
Found: Western North America, Portugal

Stegosaurus **was declared the official state dinosaur of Colorado in 1982.**

11

JURASSIC GIANTS

They were the largest animals that have ever lived on land. With their long necks, sauropods could reach plants and leaves, which they gobbled down whole. *Brachiosaurus* (opposite) held its neck upright like a giraffe's so it could reach high trees. *Diplodocus* (below) stood with its neck straight out so that it could poke into forests to scoop up ferns, leaves, and soft plants.

The Real Poop

Sauropods were giant eating machines, chomping constantly on ferns and conifer needles. All of this eating produced lots of dung that mostly got trampled into the ground. But some of it became fossils called *coprolites*. Since sauropods were so huge they must have produced giant-sized poop, right? Not so. Scientists believe that their dung was pellet-sized, rather like that of an elk. *Coprolites* from carnivores are larger. This petrified poop (below) from a *T. rex* weighs about 15 pounds.

DIPLODOCUS was longer than two school buses and had a long tail that it could crack like a bullwhip. It walked on four legs the size of tree trunks, and each foot had a sharp thumb claw that may have been used for fighting. *Diplodocus* babies were hatched from eggs and may have lived for as long as 50 years.

Name Means: "Double beamed." Its spine had double-pronged bones that may have helped keep its long tail off the ground
Size: Up to 115 feet long, with a 20-foot neck and a 46-foot tail
Weight: 11–17.6 tons
Time: 154–144 million years ago
Diet: Plants
Found: Colorado, Utah, Montana, and Wyoming

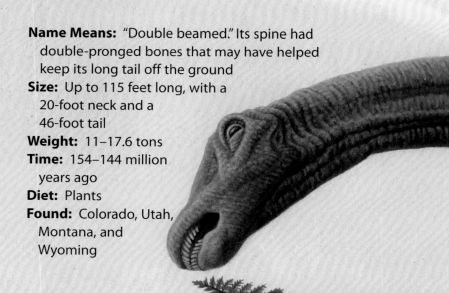

BRACHIOSAURUS needed a very powerful heart to pump blood up its long neck to its brain (even though it had a relatively small brain, like most sauropods). Scientists think a brachiosaur's blood pressure must have been three or four times as high as ours. Unlike *Diplodocus*, a brachiosaur had a short, thick tail and front legs that were longer than its hind legs.

Name Means: "Arm lizard"
Size: Up to 82 feet long and 42 feet tall
Weight: 35–41 tons
Time: 154–144 million years ago
Diet: Plants
Found: Western North America, Africa

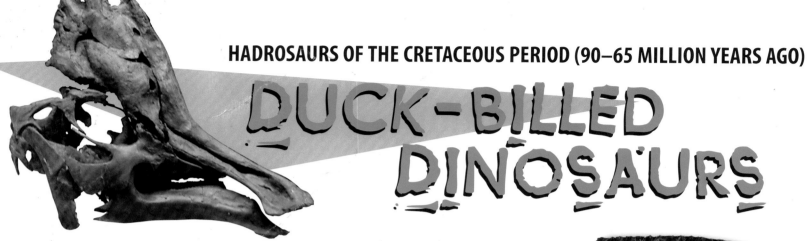

DUCK-BILLED DINOSAURS

Hadrosaurs were once the most common dinosaurs in North America. They had wide, toothless beaks that looked like a duck's bill. Their beaks were good for nipping off plants that were then chewed by an amazing set of teeth. An adult human has 32 teeth. A hadrosaur had as many as 200 — with three to five replacements stacked underneath each one!

This piece of a hadrosaur's jaw shows its many teeth. As each tooth wore down, a new one was right there to replace it.

There were two main kinds of hadrosaurs. Some had flat skulls and were plainer-looking, while others had strange head crests like the one on *Corythosaurus,* seen opposite. These hollow crests came in many different shapes and were probably used to create noises that could attract mates or warn others of danger. Their ability to live together and protect each other was likely an important factor in the success of the hadrosaurs. Toward the end of the Cretaceous period, as the number of dinosaurs declined, hadrosaurs were among the survivors.

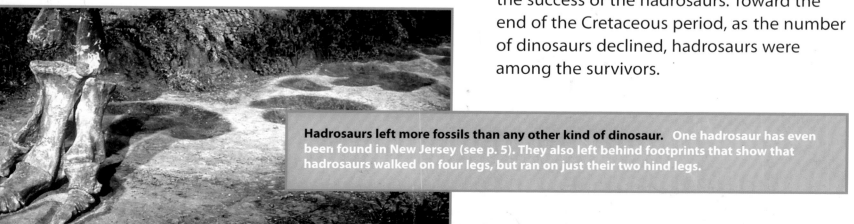

Hadrosaurs left more fossils than any other kind of dinosaur. One hadrosaur has even been found in New Jersey (see p. 5). They also left behind footprints that show that hadrosaurs walked on four legs, but ran on just their two hind legs.

Some corythosaurs ("helmet lizards") pass through
an ancient forest. They were about 30 to 33 feet
long and weighed up to 5 tons.

LIFE AMONG THE CRESTED DUCKBILLS

Lambeosaurus
had a forward-leaning head crest that may have been used to attract mates.

LAMBEOSAURUS

was one of the biggest crested duckbills, growing as long as a city bus at 50 feet, though most specimens found are only 30 to 40 feet long. A baby lambeosaur had no crest. As it grew, the nasal bones in its skull expanded to form the tall, hollow crest. And like *Corythosaurus*, it may have made a sound through its crest. Its weight was approximately that of a pickup truck — 3.3 tons. *Lambeosaurus* was named for paleontologist Lawrence Lambe in 1923. Bones of a huge, 50-foot lambeosaur have been found in Baja California, Mexico.

PARASAUROLOPHUS had perhaps the most spectacular crest of all the hadrosaurs. It was hollow and bony and could be up to 6 feet long. There was a notch where the end of the crest touched the creature's back. The crest had four tubes inside it that may have been used to produce a low sound, like the one a foghorn makes. Scientists believe that each species of *Parasaurolophus* may have made a distinctive sound that others could recognize. Fossils show us that it had a pebbly-textured hide, and it is often depicted with colored skin. We don't know exactly what color dinosaurs were, but we assume that some of them had beautiful colors, like modern lizards. From its beak to its pointed tail, *Parasaurolophus* was 31 to 39 feet long, and at 2.7 to 3.8 tons could weigh as much as an elephant.

Hadrosaurs had leathery skin that was smoother on their bellies. They may have had varying skin colors, too.

Parasaurolophus fossils have been found in Utah, New Mexico, and Alberta, Canada. *Parasaurolophus* lived 76 to 73 million years ago.

MAIASAURA had no fancy crest, though it did have a bony knob between its eyes. Its name means "good mother lizard," because when its bones were first found they were lying near nests with the remains of babies. To make a nest, the mother *Maiasaura* would scoop a hole in the ground and lay about 25 grapefruit-sized eggs in it. She would then spread sand over her eggs and cover them with leaves and plants. As the plants rotted, they would keep the eggs warm. The newly hatched babies were about 12 inches in length (above), but an adult *Maiasaura* would grow to be roughly 30 feet long. In Montana, 10,000 *Maiasaura* fossils have been found together. This indicates that they likely lived in large herds and migrated with the seasons.

FLAT-SKULLED HADROSAURS

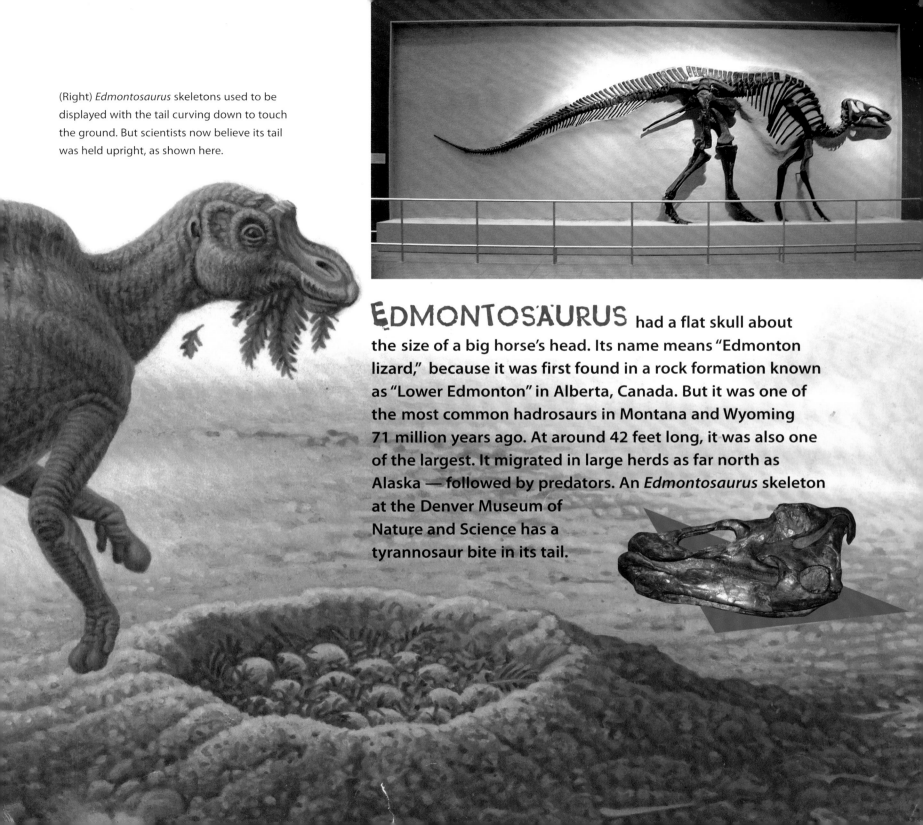

(Right) *Edmontosaurus* skeletons used to be displayed with the tail curving down to touch the ground. But scientists now believe its tail was held upright, as shown here.

EDMONTOSAURUS had a flat skull about

the size of a big horse's head. Its name means "Edmonton lizard," because it was first found in a rock formation known as "Lower Edmonton" in Alberta, Canada. But it was one of the most common hadrosaurs in Montana and Wyoming 71 million years ago. At around 42 feet long, it was also one of the largest. It migrated in large herds as far north as Alaska — followed by predators. An *Edmontosaurus* skeleton at the Denver Museum of Nature and Science has a tyrannosaur bite in its tail.

HERDS OF HORNS

Huge herds of horned and frilled dinosaurs once lumbered across North America. *Triceratops* is one of the most famous of them. But 14 different kinds of horned dinos (called ceratopsians) have been found in the western U.S. and Canada. All of them were four-footed plant eaters and had bulky bodies, short tails, and parrot-like beaks. Each species had a different-shaped frill topped by horns and spikes. The frills of most horned dinosaurs were too thin to have given much protection from an attack by a predator such as *T. rex*. But the 3-foot-long horns on the elephant-sized *Triceratops* are known to have caused damage when used in a fight.

CHASMOSAURUS

had the showiest frill of all, with large holes, or "chasms," in it. Scientists now believe these frills were mainly used for display during mating season — like a wild turkey fanning its tail in spring. So its frill may well have been brightly colored, as shown here. Dinosaurs probably had eyes that could see in color, like birds do today.

TRICERATOPS

was among the largest and most common dinosaurs of its time. Scientists have discovered as many as 200 *Triceratops* skulls in one rock formation in Montana. This dino had one horn on its snout, two longer ones above its eyes, and a solid neck frill. (When the first *Triceratops* bones were found in 1887 near Denver, Colorado, the discoverers thought they might have belonged to an ancient buffalo.) *Triceratops* was also one of the last dinosaurs to become extinct.

Name Means:
  "Three-horned face"
Size: 26–29.5 feet long and
  up to 9.8 feet tall
Weight: 6–13 tons
Time: 68–65 million years ago

Diet: Plants
Found: Western North America

STYRACOSAURUS

had four to six long spikes jutting from its frill, two above its eyes, and a 2-foot-long horn pointing up from its snout. Styracosaurs likely traveled in herds and may have formed into a spiky circle to protect their young from attackers.

Name Means: "Spiked lizard"
Size: Up to 18 feet long
  and 6 feet tall
Weight: Up to 3 tons

Time: 76.5 to 75 million years ago
Diet: Plants
Found: Western North America

WALKING TANKS

PANOPLOSAURUS ("armored lizard") was one of the more common ankylosaurs 74 million years ago. It was about 15 feet long and could weigh up to 3 tons. Four large spikes jutted down from its shoulders. These may have been used in contests of strength with other ankylosaurs. For protection, it probably crouched down to guard its underbelly. *Panoplosaurus* had a long, flat skull with small teeth and weak jaws, which limited its diet to soft plants like ferns. Fossils from it have been found in Montana, South Dakota, Texas, and Alberta, Canada.

They waddled along looking like armored tanks. Bony armor, studs, and spikes gave them protection — some of them even had armored eyelids! *Euoplocephalus*, seen below, was one of the largest ankylosaurs — about the size of a minivan. Only when flipped over could it be wounded.

EUOPLOCEPHALUS

Name Means: "True plated head"
Size: Up to 19.6 feet long
Weight: 2 tons
Time: 76.5–69 million years ago

Diet: Low-lying plants
Found: Western North America

Euoplocephalus's **bony tail club could weigh up to 66 pounds. It was a mean wrecking ball and would likely have broken the leg of any attacking tyrannosaur.**

PHEW!

Did an Ankylosaur Pass Here?

Ankylosaurs had to eat many low-lying plants with tough stems, which likely fermented in their large guts — producing lots of

SMELLY GAS!

FEATHERS & CLAWS

Did birds evolve from dinosaurs?

Most scientists think they did. Birds first appeared about 150 million years ago. Their ancestors were small dinosaurs that had three-toed feet and hollow bones, and sat on nests — just like birds. They were relatives of the dromaeosaurs, a group of dinosaurs that later included *Velociraptor* (above), *Bambiraptor* (below), and *Utahraptor* (opposite). Although they weren't birds, these dinosaurs did have feathers and claws.

The similar bone structures of *Bambiraptor* and a modern-day roadrunner show why scientists think birds evolved from dinosaurs.

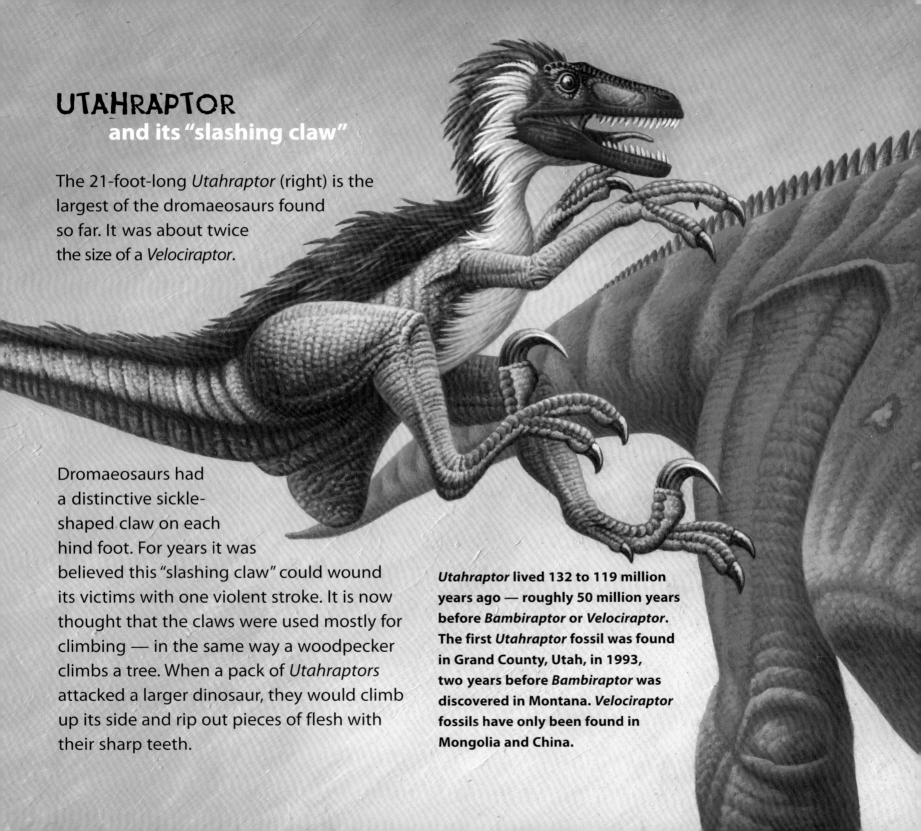

UTAHRAPTOR
and its "slashing claw"

The 21-foot-long *Utahraptor* (right) is the largest of the dromaeosaurs found so far. It was about twice the size of a *Velociraptor*.

Dromaeosaurs had a distinctive sickle-shaped claw on each hind foot. For years it was believed this "slashing claw" could wound its victims with one violent stroke. It is now thought that the claws were used mostly for climbing — in the same way a woodpecker climbs a tree. When a pack of *Utahraptors* attacked a larger dinosaur, they would climb up its side and rip out pieces of flesh with their sharp teeth.

Utahraptor lived 132 to 119 million years ago — roughly 50 million years before *Bambiraptor* or *Velociraptor*. The first *Utahraptor* fossil was found in Grand County, Utah, in 1993, two years before *Bambiraptor* was discovered in Montana. *Velociraptor* fossils have only been found in Mongolia and China.

With an eerie, brilliant light, it lit up the sky. The flaming asteroid then slammed into the earth, blasting enormous chunks of rock into the air. Earthquakes, dust clouds, and acid rain followed, wiping out more than half of all the plants and animals on earth — including the dinosaurs.

But is the "killer asteroid" the *only* reason the dinosaurs became extinct? Most scientists think it was just the last straw.

65 MILLION YEARS AGO

WIPEOUT!

By the time the asteroid crashed into Mexico, the shallow seas that once covered the Great Plains had dried up. The lush deltas where the hadrosaurs had nibbled on flowering plants were gone. The climate had become cooler, and many dinosaurs may not have survived the colder winters.

To make matters worse, huge volcanoes had erupted in different parts of the world during these years. Plants and animals would have suffered from the massive clouds of volcanic ash and poisonous gas.

So when the asteroid struck, the dinosaurs that were left were finished off. Perhaps if it had landed in an earlier time, some of them might have survived.

But the dinosaurs that evolved into birds *did* survive. From small, ancient dinosaurs came the 9,300 kinds of birds that we know today. And when you look at an ostrich or the claws of a woodpecker, you can see that dinosaurs are not only found in museum displays. They are with us still.

The asteroid hit near the Yucatán Peninsula of Mexico. Craters from the explosion have been found thousands of miles away. Below, a *Triceratops* dies in a forest fire caused by the flaming asteroid.

WHEN THE DINOSAURS RULED

TRIASSIC:
250–200 million years ago

JURASSIC:
200–145 million years ago

CRETACEOUS:
145–65 million years ago

TODAY

First single cell
3.5 billion
years ago

Blue-green
algae

Wormlike organisms
with spinal cords

Jawless fish

Land plants

Amphibians

Reptiles

PALEOZOIC ERA
540–250 million years ago

Pronunciation Guide

Allosaurus: **AL oh SORE us**

Ammosaurus: **AM oh SORE us**

ankylosaur: **an KIE loh SORE**

Bambiraptor: **BAM bee RAP tore**

Brachiosaurus: **brake e oh SORE us**

ceratopsians: **SER uh TOP see ins**

Chasmosaurus: **KAZ moh SORE us**

Corythosaurus: **koh RITH oh SORE us**

Diplodocus: **dip PLOD oh kuss**

dromaeosaurs: **DROH mee oh SORES**

Edmontosaurus: **ed MON toh SORE us**

elasmosaur: **eh LAZZ mo SORE**

Eubrontes: **yoo BRON tees**

Euoplocephalus: **YOO oh ploh SEF uh lus**

Gorgosaurus: **GOR go SORE us**

hadrosaur: **HAD roh SORE**

Hadrosaurus: **HAD roh SORE us**

Hesperornis: **Hes per ORN is**

Hypacrosaurus: **hye PACK ro SORE us**

Lambeosaurus: **LAM bee oh SORE us**

Maiasaura: **my ah SORE ah**

mosasaur: **MOZ ah SORE**

Panoplosaurus: **PAN oh plo SORE us**

Parasaurolophus: **PAR ah sore AWL loff us**

sauropods: **SORE oh pods**

Stegosaurus: **steg oh SORE us**

Styracosaurus: **stie RAK oh SORE us**

Triceratops: **trye SAIR a tops**

Tyrannosaurus: **tye RAN oh SORE us**

Utahraptor: **YOO tah RAP tore**

Velociraptor: **vel OSS ih RAP tore**

Xiphactinus: **zie FAK tin us**

The first dinosaurs lived approximately 220 million years ago, during the Triassic period. The last of them were gone by the end of the Cretaceous period, 65 million years ago. The early dinosaurs lived on a single land mass called Pangaea, a "supercontinent" that separated over time to yield the modern continents. During the Jurassic and Cretaceous periods, Earth's continents drifted farther and farther apart until the globe finally resembled the world we know today.

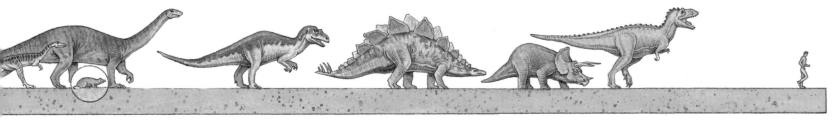

early dinosaurs   Mammals   *Allosaurus*   *Stegosaurus*   *Triceratops*   *Tyrannosaurus rex*   Modern humans
                                                                                                                               200,000 years ago

MESOZOIC ERA
250–65 million years ago

Glossary

asteroid: a celestial body that is smaller than a planet but larger than a meteorite and that usually orbits around the sun

coprolite: fossilized excrement

dinosaurs: Land-dwelling animals that lived on Earth from 225 to 65 million years ago. Their legs were right under their bodies and did not stick out from their sides like a lizard's. Not all ancient creatures were dinosaurs, especially not those that swam or flew.

Mesozoic: The scientific name for the era during which the dinosaurs lived. It is divided into three periods: the **Triassic** (250–200 million years ago), the **Jurassic** (200–145 million years ago), and the **Cretaceous** (145–65 million years ago).

paleontologist: a scientist who studies life in prehistoric times

sickle: a tool with a curved blade and short handle used for cutting grass or wheat

Recommended Reading

Dinomummy: The Life, Death and Discovery of Dakota, a Dinosaur from Hell Creek
by Dr. Phillip Lars Manning, foreword by Tyler Lyson. Houghton-Mifflin, 2007. *The story of a mummified dinosaur's life, death, and rediscovery.*

National Geographic Dinosaurs
by Paul Barrett. National Geographic, 2001. *A good overview of 50 dinosaurs with 300 illustrations.*

The Best Book of Dinosaurs
by Christopher Maynard. Kingfisher, 2005. *An easy introduction to the world of dinosaurs with many pictures.*

WHERE TO SEE DINOSAURS

U.S. MUSEUMS

Academy of Natural Sciences, Philadelphia In Dinosaur Hall see *Hadrosaurus foulkii*, found in 1878, and more than 30 other species. www.ansp.org

American Museum of Natural History, New York Visit one of the world's greatest collections of ancient fossils. www.amnh.org

Buffalo Museum of Science In "Dinosaurs & Co." stand face-to-face with *T. rex*, *Triceratops*, *Allosaurus*, and others. www.sciencebuff.org

Carnegie Museum of Natural History, Pittsburgh "Dinosaurs in Their Time" shows dinosaurs in accurate re-creations of their environments with plants and other creatures. www.carnegiemnh.org

Cleveland Museum of Natural History Kirtland Hall has an *Allosaurus* skeleton and many other ancient fossils. www.cmnh.org

Denver Museum of Nature and Science In "Prehistoric Journey" see *Allosaurus* and *Stegosaurus* do battle. www.dmns.org

Exhibit Museum of Natural History, University of Michigan, Ann Arbor The Hall of Evolution has dinosaurs, ancient whales, and more. www.lsa.umich.edu

The Field Museum, Chicago Meet Sue, the world's most famous *T. rex*, and many other dinosaurs in interactive displays. www.fieldmuseum.org

Fort Worth Museum of Science Explore species from Texas's prehistoric past. www.fwmuseum.org

Harvard Museum of Natural History, Cambridge, Mass. The zoological galleries include the world's only mounted *Kronosaurus*, a 42-foot-long prehistoric marine reptile. www.hmnh.harvard.edu

Houston Museum of Natural Science The Hall of Paleontology contains more than 450 fossils, including a *T. rex*. www.hmns.org

Museum of the Rockies, Montana State University, Bozeman Famed paleontologist Jack Horner is a curator at this important dinosaur museum that has many fossils and exhibits, including the biggest *T. rex* skull in the world. www.museumoftherockies.org

Natural History Museum of Los Angeles County See paleontology in action at the "Thomas the *T. rex* Lab" while Dinosaur Hall is under renovation — it is scheduled to reopen in 2011. www.nhm.org

New Mexico Museum of Natural History, Albuquerque Learn about Triassic New Mexico in "Dawn of the Dinosaurs." See two giant Jurassic creatures locked in combat, and other great dinosaur displays. www.nmnaturalhistory.org

Peabody Museum of Natural History, Yale University, New Haven, Conn. See the *Ammosaurus major* from Connecticut, a *Stegosaurus*, and other skeletons. www.peabody.yale.edu

Smithsonian National Museum of Natural History, Washington, D.C. Some of the oldest and most important dinosaur skeletons ever found are here — including an 80-foot-long *Diplodocus*. www.mnh.si.edu

Sternberg Museum of Natural History, Hays, Kansas Discover the marine reptiles that once swam over Kansas. www.fhsu.edu/sternberg

University of Wyoming Geological Museum, Laramie See "Big Al" the *Allosaurus* and other great specimens. www.uwyo.edu

Utah Museum of Natural History, University of Utah, Salt Lake City Watch curators preparing fossils and learn about Utah's first *T. rex*, plus hadrosaurs and ceratopsians. www.umnh.utah.edu

U.S. PARKS

Dinosaur State Park, Rocky Hill, Conn. Beneath a geodesic dome see 200-million-year-old dinosaur tracks. www.dinosaurstatepark.org

INDEX

Page numbers in bold italic
refer to illustrations.

**Dinosaur National Monument,
Jensen, Utah** Explore where dinosaurs
lived and died. www.nps.gov/dino

**Petrified Forest National Park,
Holbrook, Arizona** Visit one of the
world's largest concentrations of
ancient petrified wood and see displays
of 225-million-year-old fossils.
www.nps.gov/pefo

CANADA

**Dinosaur Provincial Park,
Patricia, Alberta** This world heritage
site east of Calgary offers hikes and
tours to fossil sites.
www.cd.gov.ab.ca/parks/dinosaur

Royal Ontario Museum, Toronto
In the spectacular new Temerty galleries,
over 40 dinosaur specimens are on
display. www.rom.on.ca/exhibitions/
nhistory/dinosaurs.php

**Royal Tyrrell Museum, Drumheller,
Alberta** One of the world's great
dinosaur museums, with hundreds of
dinosaur fossils and displays.
www.tyrrellmuseum.com

For a list of even more dinosaur sites
and museums go to:
paleobiology.si.edu/dinosaur/
collection/where/north_america.html

Selected Bibliography

Everhart, Michael J. *Oceans of Kansas*. Bloomington: Indiana University Press, 2005

Fastovsky, David E. and Weishampel, David B. *The Evolution and Extinction of the Dinosaurs*, 2nd Edition. Cambridge: Cambridge University Press, 1996

Funston, Sylvia. *The Dinosaur Question and Answer Book*. Toronto: Greey de Pencier, 1992

Gardom, Tim and Milner, Angela. *The Natural History Museum Book of Dinosaurs*. London: Carlton Books, 2007

Grady, Wayne. *The Dinosaur Project*. Toronto: Macfarlane, Walter & Ross, 1993

Reid, Monty. *The Last Great Dinosaurs*. Red Deer: Red Deer College Press, 1990

Royal Tyrrell Museum. *Reading the Rocks: A Biography of Ancient Alberta*. Calgary: Red Deer Press, 2003

Russell, Dale A. *The Dinosaurs of North America*. Toronto: University of Toronto Press, 1989

Sattler, Helen Roney. *Dinosaurs of North America*. New York: Lothrop, Lee and Shepard, 1981

Spalding, David. *Into the Dinosaur's Graveyard*. Toronto: Doubleday, 1999

Stewart, Ron. *Dinosaurs of the West*. Edmonton: Lone Pine Publishing, 1988

Wallace, Joseph. *The Rise and Fall of the Dinosaur*. New York: Mitchell Friedman, 1987

Weishampel, David B. and Young, Luther. *Dinosaurs of the East Coast*. Baltimore: Johns Hopkins University Press, 1996

Credits and Acknowledgements

All illustrations are by Alan Barnard and all fossils and skeletons are from the collection of the Royal Ontario Museum with the exceptions of: (p. 9) *Xiphactinus*, Triebold Paleontology Inc.; (p. 12) *T. rex coprolite*, Royal Saskatchewan Museum; (p. 11) *Stegosaurus* model by Stephen Czerkas, copyright 1986. The chart and diagrams on pp. 28–29 are by Jack McMaster. We would like to thank Janet Waddington at the Royal Ontario Museum for her advice and assistance and also curators David Evans and Kevin Seymour for their time and expertise. Thanks also to Brian Porter, Nicola Woods, Scott Auerbach, Chad Beckerman, and Tamar Brazis.

Library of Congress Cataloging-in-Publication Data

Brewster, Hugh.
Dinosaurs in your backyard / by Hugh Brewster ; illustrated by Alan Barnard.
p. cm.
Includes bibliographical references and index.
ISBN 978-0-8109-7099-1 (Harry N. Abrams : alk. paper)
1. Dinosaurs—North America—Juvenile literature. I. Barnard, Alan, ill.
II. Title.
QE861.5.B74 2009
567.9097—dc22
2008030406

Developed in cooperation with the Royal Ontario Museum with the generous support of the Louise Hawley Stone Charitable Trust.

Illustrations copyright © 2009 Alan Barnard
Text copyright © 2009 Hugh Brewster
Compilation © Whitfield Editions
Produced by Whitfield Editions
Art Director: Gord Sibley

Printed and bound in China
10 9 8 7 6 5 4 3 2 1

Abrams Books for Young Readers are available at special discounts when purchased in quantity for premiums and promotions as well as fundraising or educational use. Special editions can also be created to specification. For details, contact specialmarkets@hnabooks.com or the address below.

HNA ◼◻◼◼◼◻
harry n. abrams, inc.
a subsidiary of La Martinière Groupe
115 West 18th Street
New York, NY 10011
www.hnabooks.com